Skyler
the Fireworks
Fairy

Special thanks to Kristin Earhart

Copyright © 2016 by Rainbow Magic Limited.

All rights reserved. Published by Scholastic Inc., *Publishers since 1920.* SCHOLASTIC and associated logos are trademarks and/or registered trademarks of Scholastic Inc. RAINBOW MAGIC is a trademark of Rainbow Magic Limited. Reg. U.S. Patent & Trademark Office and other countries. HIT and the HIT logo are trademarks of HIT Entertainment Limited.

The publisher does not have any control over and does not assume any responsibility for author or third-party websites or their content.

No part of this publication may be reproduced, stored in a retrieval system, or transmitted in any form or by any means, electronic, mechanical, photocopying, recording, or otherwise, without written permission of the publisher. For information regarding permission, write to Scholastic Inc., Attention: Permissions Department, 557 Broadway, New York, NY 10012.

This book is a work of fiction. Names, characters, places, and incidents are either the product of the author's imagination or are used fictitiously, and any resemblance to actual persons, living or dead, business establishments, events, or locales is entirely coincidental.

ISBN 978-0-545-85204-3

10 9 8 7 6 5 4 3 2 1   16 17 18 19 20

Printed in the U.S.A.   40

First printing May 2016

Skyler
the Fireworks
Fairy

by Daisy Meadows

SCHOLASTIC INC.

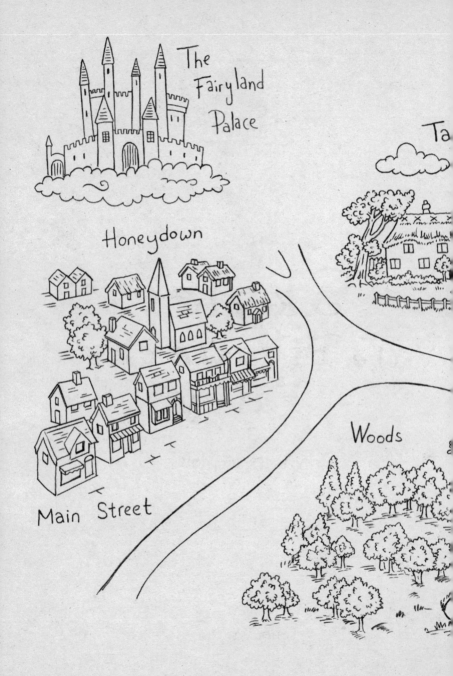

ttage

Jack Frost's
Ice Castle

Playground

Honeydown Lake

Everyone likes to get away,
To escape for a vacation or holiday.
They go to a place that is sweet.
They take it easy, have a well-earned treat.

But I, Jack Frost, work day in and day out.
It's enough to make a dark wizard pout.
Evil magic is not always easy for me.
I want to relax and be leisurely.

I'll ruin people's customs and the joy will be mine.
Then I'll take a vacation and life will be fine.
I won't stop until the fairies all see,
That no one deserves a break more than me, me, me!

**Find the hidden letters in the stars throughout
this book. Unscramble all 9 letters to spell a
special fireworks word!**

Cupcake
Catastrophe

Contents

Cross Your Fingers

"Quick! Cross your fingers," Kirsty
Tate declared. She gave her best friend,
Rachel Walker, a meaningful glance.
They were sitting in the backseat of the
Tates' family minivan. "You don't want
to jinx it."

Rachel nodded and they latched their
fingers together. She knew Kirsty was

right. Just because the two friends were
going away together did not mean that
they would get to have a fairy adventure.
It was true that Rachel and Kirsty had
been very lucky on vacations in the past.
Together, they had shared a lot of fairy
fun! Ever since they first met each other
on Rainspell Island, they had met all
kinds of fabulous fairies. They were even
friends with Queen Titania and King
Oberon, the kind and wise rulers of
Fairyland. The queen and king often
asked Kirsty and Rachel for help when
things went wrong in the magical realm.

"All crossed," Rachel said with a smile,
thinking about how fun it would be to
meet a new fairy on their trip to see
Kirsty's grandparents. "I know it's never
a sure thing, but we can always hope."

"Hope for what?" Mrs. Tate asked from the front seat of the car. Rachel and Kirsty looked at each other again. "You know, Mom," Kirsty answered. "We're just hoping for good weather while we're staying with Gran and Gramps."

Even though Kirsty and Rachel had helped all kinds of amazing fairies, they couldn't tell anyone about them. Kirsty didn't like to keep the truth from her parents, but the safety of Fairyland depended on it staying a secret.

Both girls were hoping to make new fairy friends, but there were lots of other

reasons to be excited for their upcoming stay with Kirsty's grandparents. First of all, it was a chance for the girls to be together. They were best friends, but they did not live in the same town or go to the same school. Also, the town of Honeydown, where Kirsty's grandparents had a country cottage, was a fascinating place with a lot of interesting history.

"Even if the weather isn't great, there are still lots of fun things to do," Kirsty's mom assured the girls. "I could spend

days in the Fireworks Factory Museum."

"Mom, you could spend days in any museum," Kirsty replied with a loving smirk,

"but that one is pretty cool. There was a famous old fireworks designer who lived in Honeydown, and the town turned his old workshop and factory into a museum," Kirsty explained to Rachel.

"Oh! I love fireworks," Rachel said. "I love the booming sound and the way the explosions vibrate in your stomach. And I love all the dazzling colors and shapes."

"Well, Rachel," Mr. Tate said, "this will be a real treat for you, because the town's birthday is this week, and there is a ton of stuff planned. There will be a cupcake social, a parade, and then a huge fireworks display on the last night."

"I can't wait!" Rachel exclaimed.

Mrs. Tate turned around and looked at them from the front seat. "You two will

have a wonderful time. I
wish we could stay the
whole week, but Gran
and Gramps will take
good care of you."

"You'll be back for
the fireworks, won't
you?" Kirsty asked.

"We wouldn't miss it," Mr. Tate
promised. "I remember the Honeydown
fireworks from when I was a kid. They're
the best!"

The next thing they knew, everyone
was piling out of the Tates' minivan
and heading to the door of a beautiful
cottage. There was a walkway with
large stepping-stones, and an ivy-covered
arch over the doorway. The roof was even
covered in grass! Rachel couldn't help

but think that it looked like something straight out of Fairyland. She was so excited to be there, it was as if tiny fireworks were going off inside her brain!

Then, as soon as she closed her car door, she thought she heard a real firework. Very tiny, but very real.

"Did you hear that?" Rachel asked Kirsty, looking around.

Kirsty shook her head.

"It sounded like a firework," Rachel whispered.

"They might be testing some, before the big celebration this weekend," Kirsty explained. She didn't seem to think it was a big deal.

Rachel nodded, but she didn't think that was it. The noise had not sounded like a large firework. It had sounded small, but very close. Something about it gave her goose bumps.

"Well, hello!" Gran and Gramps called from the open door. "Welcome!" They waved, their faces creased with bright smiles.

As Rachel went to greet Kirsty's grandparents, she convinced herself

that her ears were playing tricks on her.
After all, she hadn't been able to get
her mind off of fairies all morning.

Kirsty's grandparents led everyone
inside. They had laid out a lunch of
turkey sandwiches and potato salad,
with chocolate cake for dessert.

After lunch, Rachel fiddled with her
napkin, distracted. She had heard tiny
explosions all through lunch. She was
having a hard time concentrating, and
Gran and Gramps kept asking her lots
of questions.

"We are thrilled to be sharing this
special week with you girls," Gramps
said as he dished out some extra-tall
pieces of triple-chocolate cake.

"None for me, thank you," Rachel

said. "The lunch was delicious, and I'm full right now."

Kirsty looked at her friend, concerned. Rachel had a faraway look in her eyes. Kirsty was confused. It wasn't like Rachel to turn down dessert! They both  loved tasty treats, especially after a healthy meal. "Could we please be excused?" Kirsty asked, glancing from her grandparents to her parents. "We still need to bring in our suitcases, and I'd love to show Rachel where we'll be sleeping."

"No cake for you, either?" Gramps asked, looking disappointed. "It's our favorite family recipe."

"Maybe we could have some this afternoon? It will taste especially good after we get settled in," Kirsty said. She absolutely loved chocolate cake, but she had a feeling she and Rachel should have a talk, in private.

"Of course, dear," Gran said with a sweet smile. "We're about to talk about lots of people you don't know, anyway. You know, adult stuff."

"Thank you," Kirsty said, scooting out her chair. She tapped Rachel on the shoulder, and Rachel also scooted back. "We'll be outside."

"Don't go too far," Mrs. Tate called

after they'd left the room. "Your dad
and I will have to head back before
too long."

"We won't," Kirsty assured her mom,
but then Rachel grabbed her hand,
tugged her through the door, and ran
toward the garden at full speed.

BOOM! BOOM! BOOM!

"Rachel, what is it?" Kirsty asked as the two girls raced across the lawn.

"I'm not sure," Rachel admitted when they finally came to a stop. "But something told me we just had to get outside and into the garden." Rachel tried to catch her breath. "I just couldn't sit there anymore."

"I understand. I started to feel the same way," Kirsty shared. "It was like I could hear tiny explosions in my head all through lunch. Is that what you were talking about when we first got here?"

"Do they start with a soft fizzing sound and then get louder?" Rachel asked.

Kirsty nodded.

"I think we're both hearing the same thing! I'm glad it's not just in my head," Rachel said. "I think they're coming from over there." Rachel motioned to a large collection of garden gnomes that decorated the south end of the yard.

"Oh, they're so funny," Kirsty said, admiring their brightly colored hats

and round faces. "Gran has so many gnomes now!"

The two friends hurried toward the garden gnomes. "The fizzing is getting louder," Rachel said.

The tallest gnome had a lopsided grin and polka-dotted suspenders. Kirsty noticed a faint stream of sparkles beginning to shoot up from his pointy red hat.

Kirsty looked at her friend. Rachel gave her an encouraging smile. Kirsty reached out. Just as her hand brushed against the garden gnome, a series of tiny, sparkling fireworks erupted into the air. *BOOM! BOOM! BOOM!*

As soon as the fireworks dissipated, a small fairy appeared, her glittery wings lifting her into the air. The wand she held was spouting rainbow sparkles that lit up like fireworks. The fairy looked sporty and fun in red capri pants, and a purple-and-white striped shirt. Her light-brown skin practically glowed, and her wavy brown hair cascaded past her shoulders.

"Hooray! You're here!" the fairy cheered. "I was getting worried, waiting so long, but all my friends back in Fairyland said I could count on you. It's my pleasure to

finally meet you, Kirsty
and Rachel. My name is
Skyler the Fireworks Fairy."

The girls took turns
introducing themselves.
Finally, Kirsty asked the
question that was on both
their minds. "Skyler, what
are you doing here in
Honeydown?" she wondered.

Kirsty and Rachel exchanged looks of
concern. "Is Jack Frost up to his old tricks
again?" The girls could hardly count the
times they'd had to go up against him
and his troublemaking goblins.

"You guessed it!" Skyler announced,
pointing her wand at Kirsty. "It all
started when he complained about being
tired and bored. One of his goblins

suggested that he might need a vacation. Jack Frost really liked the idea." Skyler put her hands on her hips, and a scowl replaced the smile on her face. "Now, there's nothing wrong with taking vacations, but there's nothing right about what Jack Frost and the goblins did next. Here, you can see for yourself. My magic bubble will replay the important scenes for us."

Skyler lifted her wand, and out burst a pale blue firework that grew to the size of a large puddle. When the sparkles faded, a clear bubble was in its place. Inside the bubble was a picture. Kirsty

and Rachel recognized the location at once. They were staring at the inside of Jack Frost's Ice Castle! Jack Frost was listening closely to one of the goblins.

"I miss the vacations I took when I was little," the goblin pouted, his green face mopey. "We'd go to small towns, and there would be candy and gift shops, funny parades in the town square, and a lot of time to just run around and be silly."

The girls watched the bubble. Inside, Jack Frost nodded his head as the goblin continued. Just then, another goblin spoke up. "Yes! I love how they'd have all kinds of little traditions that made everything seem fun. Like bird-watching every Saturday morning and eating toasted bogmallows right after!"

Rachel and Kirsty looked at each other uncertainly. The girls couldn't picture a noisy goblin going bird-watching. They'd scare away all the birds! But the other goblins soon started to get excited, too. "Yes! We need reminders of all the fun stuff. Parades! Decorations! Sweet treats! The stuff that makes little celebrations feel festive!"

"That's it!" Jack Frost exclaimed. "I want to go to a place that lets me

feel like a kid
again!"

"That's funny,"
Kirsty said.
"That's exactly
how my grandparents
describe Honeydown."

"Exactly," Skyler said, hovering over
the girls' shoulders. "That's why they are
all here. It sounds fine, right? Almost
sweet, but then they had to be selfish
and ruin it." The picture in the magic
bubble quickly changed. Now it showed
a cozy toadstool cottage with a red
polka-dotted roof. "That's my house,"
Skyler explained. "And those goblins
were not invited."

Rachel and Kirsty gasped as they
watched what happened next. The goblins

snuck into the house and stole three items, one by one.

"Jack Frost sent them after my three magic objects, because he wanted to make sure he would have the most perfect vacation getaway ever. As the Fireworks Fairy, it's my job to protect life's little traditions. I'm in charge of all those things that the goblins were just talking about!" Skyler's tiny hands closed into fists and she shook them. "But my magic doesn't really work if I don't have the objects. I can't help make things festive and fun, and I can't keep things from going horribly wrong."

All at once, the bubble picture popped.

"Oh, great!" Skyler complained. "Now that's not working, either."

"Don't worry." Rachel quickly comforted the fairy. "I think we got the idea. The goblins are trying to create a cozy, fun vacation for Jack Frost, so they stole your magic objects."

"Yes," Skyler said with a sigh. "And when I tried to stop them, Jack Frost suddenly appeared and created a whirlwind of icy magic. That wind picked up all the goblins and sent them into the human world, so it would be harder for me to find them."

"You think the goblins are here? In Honeydown?" Kirsty asked, looking around nervously.

"Yes, and they have my objects.

Will you help me find them?" Skyler asked.

Kirsty and Rachel agreed at once. It sounded like they had another fairy mission!

"Why do they need the magic objects?" Rachel wondered. "Why can't Jack Frost just go on vacation without bothering anyone else?"

"That's a good question," Skyler said. "I'm not sure what he has planned. But I do know that until we get my objects back, the fun traditions of vacation will be ruined for everyone!"

The Missing Magic

"OK," Skyler began. Her tone had suddenly turned very businesslike. "As you know, there isn't much time. This whole week is jam-packed with fun events in Honeydown. As long as the goblins have my objects, anything could go wrong." The fairy paced in midair,

her wings fluttering in time to an imaginary military march.

Kirsty and Rachel listened closely as Skyler filled them in on the details of their task.

"First, we need to find my magic cupcake," Skyler explained. "You know how you need to follow a recipe to make a great cake?" The girls nodded. "You also need to have a plan for traditions. Without thinking things through, they won't turn out they way you want them, and then no one will be happy."

"That makes sense," Kirsty said. "We'll try to find that first."

"What are the other magic objects?" Rachel asked. "Just so we'll be prepared."

"The second is a
string of bunting,"
answered Skyler.

"Bunting? What's
that?" Kirsty wondered.

"You've seen bunting before," Skyler
assured her. "Bunting is all those strings
of cute, colorful triangles hanging
around town. Bunting is often used at the
opening of a new store, or a used-car lot."

"Oh, I love that!"
Kirsty responded.
"It looks so happy.
I just never knew
its name before."

"And the last object is
my magic sparkler," Skyler
said. "You'll be able to tell
it's mine because it never goes out."

Both girls nodded, feeling relieved that they had a plan for rescuing everyone's fun-filled vacation celebrations.

"Now, if you don't mind," Skyler said, "I'd like to focus on our first object. There's still a lot of planning necessary for Honeydown's birthday bash, so I want to get the magic cupcake back to Fairyland safe and sound."

"You can count on us," Rachel said confidently.

Just then, the door to the grass-roofed cottage opened. Kirsty's grandparents and parents came out. "I don't understand why you would make the cake without a recipe. That's just silly," Gran said in a playful, but scolding tone. "If it's an old family recipe, you need to follow the recipe."

Gramps didn't respond. He just shuffled around looking grumpy.

"Uh-oh," Skyler said. "It looks like the troubles are already starting."

"And it looks like my parents are leaving," Kirsty pointed out.

"Quick, Skyler, you can hide in my pocket," Rachel offered, tugging on the loose fabric of her shirt so the fairy could slip right in.

The girls hurried over and gave the Tates big hugs.

"I can't believe we won't see you until the weekend," Mrs. Tate said, kissing Kirsty on the head. "I'm sure you'll find a way to keep busy," Mr. Tate added. "I'm sure we will," Kirsty said with a giggle as she snuck a glance at the little lump in Rachel's shirt pocket.

As soon as Kirsty's parents had driven off, Gramps pulled out his own car keys. "Well, since my cake ended up tasting like stale toothpaste and cough syrup, I'm going into town. I'm still hungry, and they have the cupcake social today."

"A social? What is that?" Rachel asked.

"Well," Gramps began, "a social is a chance for lots of people to come together and share something. In this case, it is cupcakes— lots of different kinds. All of the proceeds go to a scholarship fund."

"Sounds like my kind of social," Rachel said. "Can Kirsty and I come?"

"Of course," Gramps said. "Let's go." Rachel smiled, and he jingled the keys in his hand.

"Why don't you walk, dear," Gran suggested. "There won't be many parking spaces with all the excitement in town."

"Good point," Gramps agreed. They set off, leaving Gran reading a mystery novel on the porch. "Walking into town is a good idea," he said to them. "This way, you girls will learn your way around. I imagine you'll want to do a lot of exploring on your own this week."

Kirsty and Rachel smiled at each other. That would work well for them. They'd need some freedom to track down the goblins—and Skyler's magic objects.

The three turned off the road and onto a dirt path. The path wove through a forest. The girls ducked under canopies of morning glories, staying close

to Gramps. He found a small branch on the ground and used it as a hiking stick. As he walked, he hummed.

"A cupcake social sounds like the perfect place to find the magic cupcake," Kirsty whispered.

"Yes, but won't there be yummy baked goods everywhere?" Rachel pointed out. "How will we know which one belongs to Skyler?"

"Oh, you'll know." Both girls heard the loud whisper that came from Rachel's pocket.

"Do you think one of the goblins will have it?" Kirsty

wondered. "If Jack Frost sent them here with all the objects, maybe they still have them."

"That is a possibility," Skyler confirmed as she peeked out of the pocket. "But most of the goblins are careless, and Jack Frost's icy whirlwind was full of strong magic. There's a good chance they lost hold of the objects along the way."

As they walked, Kirsty kept thinking she could see movement deep in the trees. Were goblins in the woods? Since Jack Frost's goblins were green, it wasn't easy to spot them in between the thick leaves!

Cupcake Crazy

After a while, the path became wider.
Sun reached down through the trees and
warmed the girls' shoulders. "We're almost
to town," Gramps announced. "This
path comes out right on Main Street."

The girls soon heard the voices of a
gathering. Kirsty kept her eyes out for
goblins, but she didn't see any.

"Here we are," Gramps said.

Kirsty and Rachel marveled at the Main Street scene. There were at least forty tables set up down the sidewalk and in the middle of the street. Each one had a different kind of cupcake on it. It looked like the best potluck ever!

Suddenly, Rachel was no longer full from the big lunch. "My stomach's growling," she said.

But something wasn't right. No one looked very happy. How could that be, with so many delicious treats all around?

"What do you mean, you forgot the sugar?" one woman asked another.

"I thought I knew the recipe by heart," the other answered. "I guess I didn't."

"Well, this isn't sweet in the least. It tastes like baking soda." The first woman's whole face was wrinkled up like she had eaten something sour.

The next table had a pretty strawberry tablecloth. The cupcakes were decorated with pink frosting. They looked beautiful, but the man eating one looked unhappy. "No, you cannot replace the

strawberries with tomatoes and still call them *strawberry surprise* cupcakes!" he insisted to the woman behind the table.

The man's son had started to cry. "I don't like tomatoes, Daddy," the boy claimed.

"This isn't at all like it's been in past years," Gramps noted. "It's usually crowded with happy people." The girls followed Gramps along the sidewalk. There weren't many people on the streets at all. The only people around were there to sell cupcakes. No one wanted to buy anything. Rachel had a feeling she knew why. There seemed to be something wrong with the treats at every table they passed!

Gramps and the girls passed burnt cupcakes, flat cupcakes that looked hard

as stone, and runny cupcakes that looked like swamp water.

The next group of cupcakes appeared to be in better shape, but the signs listed some not-so-tasty flavors: broccoli and chocolate; avocado and orange salt; mustard and watermelon crunch. "Nothing sounds good," Kirsty said to herself.

"I don't know," a little girl with a chef's hat told her mom. She looked hard at the trays of cupcakes she was trying to

sell. "I just thought I would switch out some of the flavors in the recipe. I was tired of making vanilla cupcakes all the time." The sign on their table said STINKY CHEESE, MUSHY MUSHROOM, and ONION CRUMBLE.

"That's too bad," Gramps whispered after they had passed the table. "I remember that family's cupcakes from other years. I always buy one. They make a wonderful, classic vanilla. They had a line all the way to the post office last year."

"What's going on?" Rachel murmured. Of course, she knew exactly what was

happening. As long as the goblins had Skyler's magic cupcake, no special traditions were in place.

"Can't you do something, Skyler?" Kirsty asked. "All this food is going to go to waste if we don't fix this soon. And the town won't make any money for the scholarship fund."

"Oh dear." Rachel sighed. "I don't think there is anything here that anyone would eat. Bacon-bubblegum cupcakes? Nacho cheese cupcakes?"

"I can't do much," Skyler admitted. "I have a little magic in my wand, but the magic objects are what really protect the traditions.

When the objects aren't in Fairyland,
none of the traditions are safe."

"Then we have to find the cupcake,
and that might mean finding the goblins,
too," Kirsty said.

"What was that, sweetheart?" Gramps
said, stopping and turning around.

"Oh," Kirsty stalled, trying to figure
out what to say to her grandfather. "I
said that I want to find a cupcake that
I can gobble up."

Gramps smiled. "I want to do the
same. There has to be at least one good
one here!"

That's when a boy bumped into
Gramps. "Oops! I'm sorry, sir," the boy
said. He looked up and tilted his baseball
cap back. "I didn't mean to run into you.
I just really want that cupcake."

"What cupcake?" Gramps asked.

The boy's brown eyes looked especially sad as he pointed to a table down the street. There was a crowd gathered, and people were jumping up and down with money in their hands. "I had to get my money. I have five dollars. I hope it's enough," the boy said. "The cupcake looks so scrumptious, with extra icing and colored sprinkles. That's my favorite."

"I wonder why so many people are crowded around that table?" Kirsty murmured to Rachel.

"I'll find out," Skyler said. In a

flash, she had zoomed out of Rachel's pocket and zipped upward to get a better look. A moment later, she fluttered back down and hid in Rachel's hair. Perched on Rachel's shoulder, she was where both girls could easily hear her. "You won't believe this," she began, "but it's the goblins. And it looks like they are selling my magic cupcake to the highest bidder!"

"W-what?" Kirsty stammered. "They can't do that! They'll ruin everything!"

Super
Delicious

"I only have four dollars," Kirsty said. "How much money do you have?" she asked Rachel.

"My parents gave me some when they dropped me off at your house," Rachel said, "but it's supposed to last all week." Rachel knew they had to get Skyler's cupcake back. It was an emergency!

But what if she needed the money for something else?

With Skyler still hiding on Rachel's shoulder, Kirsty and Rachel approached the table staffed by the goblins.

"Step right up, step right up," a goblin in a chef's hat and apron called. "Who wants the most delicious cupcake of all?" He held a sloppy, hand-painted poster that read WORLD'S BEST EVER CUPCAKE with a large arrow pointing down.

"My daughter wants it," a voice called out. The girls turned to see a man wearing a pin-striped suit stride toward the group. His hand was raised in the air. His daughter trotted next to him. Her silky braids looked golden in the sun.

"I would like it, too," the little boy

mumbled as the man hurried past. He held his five-dollar bill in both hands.

The man in the suit had taken out his wallet and was pushing his way to the front of the crowd. "Scoot, scoot," he directed the people in front of him. "Make way."

"Now, that's not right," Gramps said, fumbling around in his pocket.

Kirsty's first thought was that maybe Gramps would buy the cupcake for her, then she snapped out of it. "That cupcake

has some seriously strong magic," she said to Rachel and Skyler. "It almost made me want to buy it."

"If we're not careful, paying way too much for a cupcake is going to become the new tradition around here," Skyler warned. "We've got to get my cupcake before someone eats it! Who knows what would happen then?"

The next thing they knew, Gramps had followed the man in the suit up to the table. The goblin standing behind the cash box looked Gramps up and down. "How much money do *you* have?" he asked. He had extra-long fingers that he tapped together as he eyed Gramps.

"I'm not going to tell *you*," Gramps answered. "I'm just trying to make sure this cupcake sale is fair."

"Excuse me, sir." The man in the suit twisted the end of his mustache as he spoke. He squinted his dark eyes at Gramps. "I am going to give this boy as much money as he wants. There is nothing unfair about that."

Gramps's mouth twitched as he looked from the long-fingered goblin to the suited man.

Kirsty bit her lip. She was worried about Gramps. His thumbs were tugging on his suspenders, and he had a scowl on his face. "Now see here," he began, "is there

really only one cupcake? Because there will be a lot of disappointed people, myself included, if the only cupcake just goes to the person with the thickest wallet."

The man in the suit gave his mustache a yank.

The girls had inched close enough now to see the cupcake. It was beautiful. It seemed to glow. The frosting was thick on top of the butter-colored cake. Rachel's mouth began to water.

"The man has a point," the gentleman in the suit said, suddenly turning his gaze to the goblins. "Why is there only one cupcake? Where are the others from this batch?"

"Um," the long-fingered goblin said.

"It's one of a kind," answered the one wearing the chef's hat and apron.

"Are you trying to pull the wool over my eyes?" the man asked, his voice gruff.

Kirsty giggled. She had heard her parents use that old saying before!

The goblins looked at each other, not knowing how to respond.

"We don't have any wool," one goblin said.

"No, no wool cupcakes today," agreed the other.

"Honey, I'm not sure about these two," the man said to the girl, putting his hands on his daughter's shoulders.

"I don't think they baked that cupcake," she pouted.

"You wouldn't try to sell me a cupcake you didn't bake, would you?" the man asked the two goblins behind the table.

The goblins gulped, trying to swallow their fear. "No, no!" they insisted. Kirsty crossed her fingers hopefully. Rachel could feel Skyler fidget on her shoulder. "Just wait," she reassured the fairy. "I think we're about to get our chance."

"I don't trust them," Gramps declared.

"Nor do I," said the man in the suit.

Without a word, one of the goblins snatched up the cupcake. "Run," yelled the other. They took off down the street, dodging empty cupcake stands as they raced off.

"Cupcake imposters!" someone declared. "Let's go after them!"

Not knowing what else to do, Rachel and Kirsty started to move with the crowd of angry cupcake buyers.

"Oh, no you don't!" Gramps grabbed them each by a shoulder, barely missing Skyler with his firm grip. "You two should stay with me. The cupcake isn't that important."

But it was! Kirsty and Rachel looked at each other. What could they do?

"Gramps," Kirsty began, trying to come up with some kind of excuse, but then Rachel squeezed her hand. The goblins had turned and were running back their way.

"Skyler, can you work some magic?" Rachel whispered.

"You bet," the fairy responded.

But just as the two green figures came darting back toward the girls, another girl appeared in their path. It was the daughter of the man in the suit. She yanked her braids, put her hands on her hips, and stood her ground. "Give me that cupcake!" she roared.

The goblins did their best to come to a

stop so they didn't run into her, but the
goblin with the cupcake tripped on his
own feet and the cupcake went flying
into the air.

But so did Skyler! The girls held their
breath as she zoomed upward. One
second, the cupcake was whirling over
their heads, and then it had vanished
amid a tiny shower of blue sparkles.

"Where'd it go?" Gramps wondered
out loud.

But just as soon as the World's Best
Ever Cupcake had disappeared, dozens of
the most delicious-looking cupcakes—in
all kinds of wonderful flavors—appeared
on the tables.

Rachel and Kirsty could see a faint
cloud sprinkling fairy dust over Main
Street. "Nice work, Skyler," Kirsty
murmured.

"That was fast!" Rachel agreed.
The fairy must have already returned the
precious cupcake to Fairyland and sent
some special magic their way.

As Gramps and the girls walked
around, they were in awe. Every single
cupcake looked like the most amazing
dessert ever. The little boy had found
one that looked almost exactly like
Skyler's cupcake. He had an enormous

grin on his face as he
took his first bite.

"Now this is what I'm
talking about," Gramps
announced. He pulled
Kirsty and Rachel in for
a group hug. "This is
what I call a cupcake
social!"

Rachel and Kirsty were so excited,
they read all the signs out loud.

*"Double Trouble Chocolate; Strawberry
Cream; Salted Caramel; Lavender Lemon;
Coconut Crumble; Pumpkin Glaze; Classic
Cheesecake; Brooklyn Blackout; Red Velvet;
Marbled Madness; White Chocolate Charm;
Blueberry Blast; Chocolate Cream Cloud."*

"Would you like to try our family
favorite for free?" asked a woman

wearing a purple bandana as she placed a giant crumb of iced cake in each girl's hand. "We're so proud of our old recipe that we love to share it." The woman smiled at her son and daughter with pride.

"We helped bake it," the girl said.

"It's a family tradition," the boy added.

"Thanks!" Gramps said as he munched on the sample. "We'll take three."

He led the girls to a bench, and they all sat down so they could savor their treats. "We can't forget to take some home for Gran," Gramps reminded them. "That's our own little tradition."

The two friends smiled at each other. That was one tradition they could make sure came true!

Perfect
Parade

Contents

No Sound like Silence

"Still no sign of Skyler," Rachel said, looking out the window. "Why haven't we heard anything?"

"I don't know," Kirsty answered, shaking her head.

It had been two days since they had rescued Skyler's magic cupcake, and the

girls hadn't seen Skyler since. They both
wondered where she could be.

"What should we do today?" Rachel
asked. The sky was very gray, and the
clouds made her feel lazy.

"I'm not sure," Kirsty answered,
putting on her sneakers. "I'll
bet there are some more fun
birthday festivities for the
town happening today."

"Girls," Kirsty's
grandma called
from the kitchen.
"Breakfast is
ready!"

"One nice thing about staying with
Gran and Gramps," Kirsty said, "is they
always feed you like it's a big holiday.
Gran loves to make french toast with

strawberry sauce. She hasn't made it yet.
I bet today's the day!"

Rachel felt her stomach rumble. "That
sounds outstanding," she said. "I love
family traditions like that."

The girls hurried out of the guest
bedroom and down the hall to the dining
room, but there wasn't anyone there.

"That's funny," Kirsty said. "Gran
always has us eat breakfast in the dining
room. Maybe she set
it up at the kitchen
table."

When the girls went
into the kitchen, they
didn't see a gourmet
meal. They didn't even
see Kirsty's gran. All
they found was a note.

Grab some cereal and a banana.
Milk is in the fridge (obviously).
See you later,
Gran

"What?" Kirsty grumbled. Her feelings were a little hurt. Gran had never deserted her for breakfast before. "Where'd she go?" Kirsty quickly searched the house but did not find Gran or Gramps. "They didn't even say good-bye," she mumbled.

"Are you thinking what I'm thinking?" Rachel asked.

"This has to be because the goblins have Skyler's other two magic objects?" Kirsty said.

"Yep," Rachel replied. "Something definitely seems fishy."

"Are you thinking what I'm thinking now?" Kirsty wondered.

"I'm thinking we should grab those bananas and get to work," Rachel said. "The big Honeydown fireworks celebration is this weekend, so there's no time to lose."

As they left the cozy grass-topped cottage, the girls went over what they knew about the situation with the goblins and Jack Frost.

"There were three missing objects. We found the first one, the magic cupcake, in town during the cupcake social," Rachel said.

"So there are still two magic objects missing," Kirsty added. "One is the bunting, the decoration with all the colorful triangles hanging from it.

The other is a sparkler that doesn't
go out." The girls headed toward the
path they had taken with Gramps earlier
that week.

"Exactly," Rachel agreed. "So we are
looking for those two things, and they
could be anywhere."

Kirsty nodded. "The goblins actually
had the cupcake, so maybe they have the
other things, too," Kirsty thought out

loud. "The goblins were holding them when Jack Frost cast the spell that sent them into the human world."

"That's right," Rachel replied. "We should always watch out for those sneaky green guys."

It was very quiet as the girls made their way along the trail. "It's such a pretty day," Rachel commented. "Where is everyone? Your grandparents talked about how many kids come here on vacation. I wonder where they all are."

"Maybe they're all in town," Kirsty suggested. "Because it's Honeydown's birthday week, there are lots of things going on." But when the trail came to an

end on Main Street, the girls still didn't
see many people around. When they
passed the playground, it was empty.

"Let's check the town calendar,"
Kirsty suggested, pointing to what
looked like a large outdoor bulletin
board. It had a wooden frame with lots
of papers tacked to it.

"There's a tug-of-war contest at
11:00," Rachel said. "Fun!"

"And a parade this afternoon," Kirsty
added.

"But not much right now," Rachel
said, looking around at the quiet street
and not knowing what to do. "You
know what Queen Titania would say?"

Kirsty nodded, "Let the magic come
to you." It was the queen of Fairyland's
reminder that fairy magic would help
them out when the time was right.
"Maybe we should get a morning muffin
and wait," Kirsty said. "The bakery has
such delicious breakfast breads. I love to
go there."

The girls crossed the street and
discovered that the bakery was closing. A
man in a baker's hat had just locked the
door. "Not enough business," he grumbled,
forcing the keys in his pocket. "Everyone's

eating ice cream instead!" The man shook his fist at a shop down the street.

"That's weird," Kirsty said, striding in that direction. "That's the ice cream store."

"Even more weird, look at that line," Rachel said. "Where did all these people come from?" As they turned the corner onto Cranberry Street, the girls saw a line that went out the store and several doors down. "And why do they want ice cream at 10:00 in the morning?"

Pssst. Pssst.

"Did you hear that?"

Pssst. Pssst.

"Look! In that tree," Kirsty said. "It's Skyler!"

"Finally!" Rachel said with a happy sigh, and the two girls rushed over to greet their newest fairy friend.

Breakfast Ice Cream

"Everything's messed up," Skyler whispered. "No one is enjoying their usual traditions."

"I think ice cream for breakfast could be a good, new tradition for me," Rachel said, rubbing her stomach.

"It sounds good," Skyler agreed, "but look at the people coming out."

The girls turned and watched as several small groups exited the ice cream parlor. Everyone was carrying a single scoop of vanilla on a wafer cone, and no one appeared to be happy.

"That's odd," Kirsty said. "This is one of those fancy ice cream shops where they use homemade brownies and cookie dough and all kinds of other stuff to make exciting flavors. So why is everyone ordering vanilla?"

"That's a good question," Rachel said. "Especially if it doesn't make them happy."

"Oh, look! There's Gramps," Kirsty said, pointing to her grandpa. He was next in line to order. "Vanilla is actually his favorite, so he will be glad when he comes out." The girls and Skyler watched closely.

The clerk with the scoop shook his head. Gramps immediately left the little shop with a scowl on his face. Skyler hid in Rachel's pocket as Kirsty waved to her grandpa. "Hey, Gramps! Over here!"

Gramps skulked his way over to the girls. "Just my luck," he complained. "They

ran out of vanilla just as soon as it was my turn."

"I'm sorry, Gramps," Kirsty said. "That's no fun. But can I ask what made you come to town for ice cream in the morning?"

"I don't know," he answered with a shrug. "Gran didn't feel like making breakfast, so we were going to go to the bakery. But then that seemed boring. We do it too much. I guess I'll just go home."

Kirsty and Rachel exchanged glances.

Gran and Gramps were tired of their own favorite traditions! This was not good at all!

"But you can't go home. There's going to be a tug-of-war contest and then the parade," Kirsty reminded him.

"I watch those things every year," he said. "I don't need to see them again." With that, Gramps headed toward the path back to the cottage.

"But that's the point," Kirsty said to herself. "He does it every year and he loves it. I wanted to share some of the Honeydown festivities with him."

"I think it's a sure sign we need to find my magic objects," Skyler declared. "Any sign of the goblins?"

"No, none," Rachel replied. "But I see a whole bag of bunting!"

"They're putting up all the town decorations!" Kirsty said. "I wonder if the magic bunting is in the bag?"

"Maybe! You'll know it because it will be extra bright, and it will have a magic glow," the fairy explained with a spin.

"The bunting helps keep people excited about traditions. It keeps the traditions from growing old."

Kirsty and Rachel knew that was exactly what was wrong with Gramps. She guessed it was why all the other people showed up in town for ice cream, too. "I get it," Rachel said. "It's easy to get sick of doing the same thing all the time. But some of these traditions only come once a year. They are tons of fun!"

"You don't have to convince me,"

Skyler said. "Let's check out that
bunting."

Skyler flew a loop and landed in
Rachel's pocket again, so the girls could
approach the workers. "Can we help?"
they asked.

Volunteering was the easiest way to
get a good look at the various strands
of bunting. Using a ladder, they helped
string the colorful decorations from one
side of Main Street to the other.

"It looks like the sweetest town ever!" Rachel exclaimed.

"I wish there were some people around to see it," Kirsty said. It was like everyone who came out for ice cream had gone home, grumpy.

"Well, I wish one of those strings of bunting was magic, but none of them are," Skyler said, folding her arms while her wings flapped behind her. "How are we going to find it?"

Calling All Kids!

"What are these?" Rachel asked as they walked by boxes of sashes, masks, and crowns. There were also hanging racks full of clothes.

"They are for today's parade," Kirsty replied. "Usually, the street is crowded with people picking out their best costume by now. Everyone dresses up."

"I'm not sure there will be much of a parade today," Rachel said, looking around at the empty street.

"I agree. This town is too quiet," Kirsty said. "I think we need to try to get people out and about. It's our best chance of finding the missing objects."

"You're right," agreed Rachel. "Those goblins like to get lost in a crowd, and they love to be part of big events." Rachel looked at the empty playground 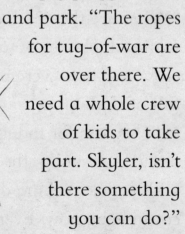 and park. "The ropes for tug-of-war are over there. We need a whole crew of kids to take part. Skyler, isn't there something you can do?"

"My wand just isn't very strong when my magic objects aren't in Fairyland," the fairy explained. "I can use it on one person, or on very small groups. But I can't send up a big sparkle cloud and get all the kids to come out at once. I'm really sorry."

"Don't worry, Skyler," Kirsty reassured the sad fairy. "There's something Rachel and I can do," Kirsty insisted. "We're going to track down some kids. This is such a fun tradition. We have to make it happen!" Kirsty ran over to the tug-of-war setup. She picked up a bright red bullhorn and pushed the button.

Rachel watched as Kirsty marched over to a row of houses. "Calling all kids! Calling all kids! Time for tug-of-war!" Kirsty yelled into the bullhorn.

At first, Rachel was embarrassed. Kirsty's voice was so loud, and no one was coming out. Then, Rachel saw inside one of the houses. A group of kids was sitting in front of a TV screen. "They're just playing video games," she mumbled to herself. Rachel actually liked video games sometimes, but not when there were other, more exciting things to do. "They could do that anytime. They should come outside! Skyler, are you with me?" With Skyler perched on her shoulder, hidden behind her hair, Rachel felt brave. She marched past the station wagon in the driveway and knocked on the door.

"Yes?" A little girl opened the door.

"Hi!" Rachel greeted her. "My name's Rachel. My friend Kirsty and I want to play tug-of-war. Will you play with us?"

Just as Rachel asked the question, Skyler sent a single stream of sparkles that swirled all around the girl. The girl's frown lifted and she smiled. "I'm Rose," she said.

Still, the little girl glanced back in the house, toward the TV room.

"It's OK, Rose," her dad called from the other room. "You should go out and play. I'll send the others."

"Thanks, Dad," she said, and she smiled again at Rachel.

"That's perfect," Skyler whispered in Rachel's ear. "If we can convince a few  kids with just a little magic, maybe a whole lot more will join us."

Happy with her success, Rachel approached other houses that looked like there might be kids at home. If there were bikes in the front yard or balls on the porch, Rachel knocked on the door. Each time, the kid looked very bored and tired. Skyler's magic always perked them right up.

"We love tug-of-war," a pair of red-headed twins declared in unison. They stormed out of their cottage and toward the park. Kirsty kept calling out on the bullhorn. Soon, kids started to show up on their own. After a little while, they had a real crowd!

Rose's father had joined the group, and he helped organize the teams. Kirsty gave the bullhorn to him. There were three ropes, and enough kids for six teams. Just right! Rachel and Kirsty noticed the little boy from earlier in the week, as well as the feisty girl with the braids. They both looked ready to compete.

Rachel and Kirsty were ready, too. Skyler was now hidden in a pocket of Kirsty's shirt. "Keep an eye out for goblins," the fairy whispered.

Luckily, the girls ended up on the same team. They took positions at the end of the rope. "I like to be anchor," Kirsty said. "It's a very important role." The girls lined up at one of the ends. The rope was braided and very thick.

The girl and the boy from the cupcake social were lined up in front of them. They introduced themselves. "I'm Sandy," said the girl with the braids.

"I'm Carter," said the boy. The red-haired twins, Milo and Arlo, were also on their team.

"The other team is all boys," Sandy said. "We'll show them." She put her hands on her hips, just like at the social.

"I don't think I know any of those kids," said Carter. "It's hard to tell, with those big bills on their baseball caps."

Big bills on baseball caps? Kirsty and Rachel had seen that before! "Goblins!" they whispered to each other. They tried to get a better view of the other team, but Rose's dad called everyone into position.

"Ready, set, tug!" he yelled.

In the anchor spot, Kirsty held tight.

Rachel was right in front of her. "Can you see them?" Kirsty grunted.

"No," Rachel responded. "We'll have to wait."

"They aren't that big," Sandy said through gritted teeth, "but they're strong."

The whole team stumbled forward, and Milo and Arlo fell across the line.

"We won! We won!" the other team all chanted together. "We are the winners, and you are the losers. We won!"

"They are not very nice winners," Carter said, looking hurt.

"No, they are not," Kirsty said, scowling at the band of big-billed and even bigger-footed bullies on the other team.

Now that she could see the other team, it was clear that they were goblins. "I think I should have a word with them." Kirsty began to march over to the group, but Rachel grabbed her by the elbow.

"Hold on," her best friend begged. "They don't know we're here yet. I think that gives us a better chance of finding the magic objects."

Skyler peeked out of Kirsty's pocket. "Can you see one of my magic objects?" she asked hopefully.

Both girls craned their necks to get better views.

"No," they both answered, shaking their heads.

"Then I think Rachel's right. Unless you can see signs of one of my magic objects, we should just keep track of the goblins. Don't go after them until you *know* they have one of my objects with them."

Kirsty looked frustrated. "What if they hid them somewhere and aren't going to bring them out?" she worried out loud. "The big firework display is tomorrow night. We have to find both objects before then, or it could be a disaster."

"That's a good point," Skyler said, scratching her chin with one finger. "But let's give this a try. If one of the objects is close, its magic will help the goblins enjoy all the fun traditions even more. I don't think they'll be able to resist taking part in all the festivities."

"You're right," Rachel agreed. "We'll just have to watch them very closely."

"We won't let them out of our sight," promised Kirsty, and she took her friend by the hand.

True Teamwork

"Great job, everyone!" Rose's father announced through the bullhorn. "Now, let's switch up the teams, just for fun."

Kirsty gave Rachel's hand a tug and the two rushed over to the other end of the rope. "Hi!" Kirsty said with a friendly wave. "We'd love to be on your team this time around. You guys are really good."

"Oh," a goblin with high cheekbones said. "Well, thank you. We just love tug-of-war. We love all these old yard games, don't we?" he said to his teammates. "Such great memories."

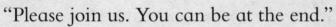

"Yes, so much fun!" said another goblin who was wearing sunglasses. "Please join us. You can be at the end."

"They're being so nice," Rachel said under her breath to Kirsty.

"They didn't seem that way when we were on the other team," Kirsty pointed out. "But they seem excited to have us on their team."

"Yes," whispered Skyler. "They are

very enthusiastic. They love the game so much, I suspect that my bunting might be close by. It helps people cherish old traditions even more."

"OK then," Kirsty said in a hushed voice. "We'll be on the lookout, and we won't give ourselves away."

"Great!" Skyler said.

All three friends felt good having a plan, but it wasn't easy pretending they didn't know who the goblins were.

Kirsty and Rachel thought it was funny that most people did not recognize that the goblins were . . . well, goblins. They were dressed like regular kids in jeans and long-sleeve sports jerseys, but

they had enormous feet, long noses, and bright green skin! Lucky for them, Jack Frost's magic helped them seem normal to people in the human world.

"New teams, please take your places," Rose's dad directed.

"Are you ready?" the high-cheeked goblin asked. "It's too bad you don't have on cleats. They keep you from slipping in the slimy mud."

"Also, we wear gloves," said another

goblin. "With gloves, the rough rope doesn't hurt our hands."

"Those are good tips," Rachel said. "We'll do our best," Kirsty added. "They really want to win,"

she said to Rachel and Skyler in a
low tone.

"That's another sign that they have the
bunting," Skyler said. "They are super
excited and well prepared. The magic
bunting helps with that."

From where she was standing, Rachel
could see almost all the goblins. There
were some who were playing tug-of-war.
Others were just cheering on the sidelines.
But no one was holding the colorful
decoration with triangles. "No sign of it
yet," Rachel said.

"Ready, set, tug!"

Rachel and Kirsty gripped the rope.
They pulled back. Without trying very
hard, they found they could take a step
back. "We're pulling the other team
over," Rachel said.

"Yes, we're winning!" Kirsty said excitedly.

"Heave," the goblins chanted in chorus. "Ho." Each time they called out, they gave a giant tug. "Heave," they chanted again. "Ho."

It seemed that they were just seconds from getting the other team across the line—and winning—when Kirsty tripped on a large root. She lost her balance and fell to the ground. Rachel tumbled on top of her. Then the goblin right in front of Rachel stumbled backward. "Yikes!" he yelled. "Grab the rope!"

But it was too late, All the goblins began to drop, one by one. And each one dropped the rope as he fell. Soon, the goblin with the high cheekbones was the last one standing. He didn't realize

that the rest of his team was out of
the game.

"Heave," he yelled all alone, but no one
else pulled. It was the other team that
managed to make a mighty yank. That
team dragged the lone goblin over the line.

Their team members gathered in a
tight huddle to celebrate.

The goblins
all scowled.
"You!" a
goblin snarled,
pointing at
Kirsty and
Rachel. "It's your fault we didn't win!"

The girls were still on the ground. "I'm
really sorry," Kirsty replied. "I tripped."

"It's more fun when we win," the
goblin pouted.

"It'll be OK," the high-cheeked goblin said. "There are other fun things to do today. It's almost time for the parade!"

"Parade?" the red-headed twins said as they passed by. They did not sound excited.

"Yes! A parade!" the goblin said, clapping his hands. "Even the pets wear costumes! You have to come! You have to dress up! Say you will?"

The twins looked at each other and raised their eyebrows. "We weren't going to go, but I guess it could be fun."

"Yes, it'll be fun! Get costumes!" The goblin ran off to recruit more kids for the parade. "Hurry up! It's almost time

to get ready for the parade! Get an outfit from home, or borrow one from the Honeydown collection!"

A quiet hum began to grow. Soon, almost everyone who had come out for tug-of-war was busy talking about their fun plans for the parade. They began to head home to get ready.

"Keep an eye on that goblin," Skyler said.

"I will," replied Rachel. "He's great! He just got everyone excited for the parade, including me!"

"Yes," answered Skyler. "That's why I think he has my bunting. Just you watch."

All Dressed Up

"Should we go home to find costumes?" Kirsty wondered. "I'll bet Gran and Gramps have some great stuff around the cottage."

"You had better stay close," Skyler insisted. "You can sort through the dress-up stuff we saw on Main Street."

"Good idea," said Rachel, and they set

off across the playground lawn. But when they arrived in the center of town, they discovered that most of the costumes had already been picked over.

"What a mess," Kirsty said, looking around. She couldn't tell what the kids in the group next to the costume rack were supposed to be. They all had on layers of jewelry and sashes and big pieces of fabric that looked like capes. The leftover clothes—once neatly hanging or placed in boxes—were scattered on the ground.

"It's a disaster," Rachel agreed, picking up a boa that didn't have many feathers left.

Both girls were wondering who would have left the costume rack in such a mess when they realized the answer was right in front of them.

"Goblins," Kirsty whispered, examining the group wearing strange costumes. When the girls looked closely, they could see the goblins' green skin under their makeup. Also, there were not a lot of dress-up shoes that fit their enormous feet. Some of the goblins were barefoot, and others still wore the cleats from the tug-of-war uniforms.

The girls looked through the remaining clothes. "There aren't any full costumes

left," Rachel noted. "We'll have to piece something together." They quickly draped cloth over their shoulders and looped belts around their waists to form togas. They tied gold scarves around their heads and put strings of gold beads around their necks. Rachel placed a single gold feather behind her ear. She gave one to Kirsty, too. "We're Greek goddesses!" they exclaimed, looking at each other.

"You look great!" Skyler said. "Now, let's track down that enthusiastic goblin. We have to figure out if he has my bunting, and how to get it back."

The girls went hand in hand through the crowd. Many goblins were fighting over necklaces or crowns. Others had buried their heads in the costume boxes, still searching.

"When is the parade supposed to start?" Rachel wondered.

"In less than an hour," Kirsty said, pointing to the old town clock in the center of the square.

"Then we don't have much time," Rachel said.

Kids and adults were starting to arrive now, so Main Street started to feel crowded.

"It's going to be harder to find him than we thought," Kirsty admitted as they searched.

"Don't worry," Skyler whispered from her hiding place in Kirsty's pocket. "Let the magic come to you."

Just as Skyler said it, the girls spotted someone dancing on the edge of the crowd, all by himself. He seemed to be waltzing. Holding one arm up and another in front of him, he took elegant sweeping steps and made graceful spins.

"It's so lovely. It looks like he is at a ball," Rachel said with admiration.

"That's our goblin!" Kirsty exclaimed in a hushed voice.

"Yes, it is!" agreed Skyler. "Check out his beautiful skirt."

When the girls looked closer, they realized that his full, many-colored skirt was the bunting! He had wrapped it around and around his waist to make a very stylish skirt that glittered with magic. As they watched, he stopped dancing and made a curtsy. He lifted the top layers of his skirt and bowed slightly. Then he began to dance again.

"He looks so happy! How will we ever get the bunting away from him?" Rachel wondered.

"I'm not sure," said Kirsty. "But the parade is about to begin."

"There's no way it will go well if we don't return the bunting to Fairyland," warned Skyler.

"How much magic do you have left in your wand?" Rachel asked Skyler.

"Just a little," Skyler admitted.

"Do you have enough to make a real costume?" Rachel asked.

Kirsty immediately understood what Rachel was thinking. "Yes!" she said. "A costume that would fit in at a real ball. A true gown!" Rachel smiled and nodded.

"Well, we can find out!" Skyler gave her wand a mighty swirl, and sparkles came out with a *whoosh!* All at once, the most gorgeous gown appeared, floating in midair! It was an elegant midnight-blue satin, with lace and ruffles on the sleeves and a full skirt that reached the floor. It

also had a wig with hair looped in a tall bun.

"Nice work!" Rachel exclaimed. "Now we just have to get the goblin to trade."

"It might not be easy," Skyler worried. "It is difficult to give up a magic object. It's part of the power."

"We'll do our best," Kirsty said, and the girls plucked the costume pieces from the air and approached the dancing goblin. Skyler crossed her fingers.

"Excuse me," Rachel began. "I am sorry to interrupt, but I couldn't help but notice your lovely dancing."

The goblin halted at once, his eyes filled with delight. "Really?" he asked.

"Yes," Kirsty responded. "Are you here for the parade?"

"Why, yes," the goblin said. "I love the chance to dress up and pretend. What a grand tradition."

"Well," said Rachel. "We were wondering if you would like to try on this special costume. It looks like it would be just your size."

The goblin reached out and touched the satin fabric. "I'm not sure," the goblin answered. "Blue isn't really my color."

The girls watched as a stream of sparkles flitted all around the dress. At once, the blue fabric changed to red. "Now, that's more like it," the goblin said and he immediately scrambled out of his old outfit and put on the dress. Then he snatched the wig from Rachel's hands.

Meanwhile, Kirsty had bent down and picked up the bunting. Skyler burst out of Kirsty's pocket. As soon as the fairy touched the colorful stringed decoration, it shrunk down to Fairyland size. In an instant, both Skyler and the bunting were gone.

The goblin didn't even notice. He was playing with the tiny curls from the wig

that fell against his neck. "Why, thank you," he said. "I will be the hit of this parade!"

Kirsty and Rachel smiled at each other. The goblin was funny; he was both polite and greedy. But above all, he was a fan of fun traditions. "Let's have a parade!" he exclaimed with a happy yell.

Suddenly, Main Street was full of people in costume and lots of people on the sidewalks, ready to cheer. Rose's dad directed everyone with the bullhorn, and soon it was time to start.

"Wow!" Kirsty said. "Skyler must have done some speedy work. Everything came together so fast!"

"That bunting must have powerful magic," Rachel said. Then, in the blink of an eye, the girls were no longer wearing their simple Greek goddess costumes. Kirsty was dressed as a pirate, complete with beard and a parrot on her shoulder. Rachel, wearing golden armor and carrying a bow and arrow, was an elf warrior. The girls smiled in disbelief.

"These are by far the coolest costumes ever!" Kirsty said.

"Coolest costumes!" the parrot repeated.

"And this will be the coolest parade," Rachel added, "because it is such a cool town tradition."

With that, the two girls took their
places with all the people, goblins, pets,
horse carriages, clowns, jugglers, and stilt
walkers. Kirsty and Rachel were happy
to enjoy the fun for now. But tomorrow,
they would have a magic sparkler to find!

Light up
the Night

Contents

Tiresome Troubles

Both Kirsty and Rachel woke early with a buzzing in their ears. Actually, it was more of a fluttering—a fluttering of fairy wings.

"Wake up, girls!" Skyler called, flitting from bed to bed. "We have a lot to do today!"

"What time is it?" Rachel wondered, rubbing her eyes.

"Is the sun even up?" Kirsty asked.

"Of course it is," Skyler said, pulling the curtain aside. A stream of bright, yellow light burst into the room.

"Barely," Kirsty insisted, putting a flowered sheet over her head. The girls were usually super excited to help their fairy friends, but they were used to a full night's sleep as well.

"It's the day of Honeydown's huge birthday celebration," Skyler declared. "The Fireworks Spectacular happens today! But it will be

spectacularly horrible if we don't find my magic sparkler."

"Do you really think the goblins are already out and about?" Rachel wondered, sitting up and stretching. "They seem kind of lazy to me."

"I never know what to expect from those green guys," Skyler said, "except trouble."

Rachel and Kirsty slowly rose to the challenge. Just as they were tying their shoes, they heard a knock at the door. "I'll get it," Kirsty offered. When she came back to the bedroom, she told Rachel that it had been the twins from tug-of-war the day before. "They want us to be part of their team. Today is the Honeydown Challenge. It's a bunch of obstacles and other games."

"It sounds like fun," Rachel said.

"And it's the perfect way for you to get out in the town," Skyler said.

"But what about the magic sparkler?" Kirsty asked. "How will we search for it if we are also taking part in the challenge?"

"No worries," Skyler said. "Always remember Queen Titania's good advice: You should let the magic come to you."

"I'm guessing there's no way the magic would come to us while we're snuggled in bed?" Kirsty asked hopefully.

"Nice try," Skyler said. "But you're already up!"

After the girls ate some of Gran's delicious french toast, they headed out to find the twins in the town center. Small groups of kids were already gathering. In the late morning sun,

Rachel thought they looked like little clusters of toadstools.

"That's so silly." Kirsty laughed when her friend mentioned it. "You definitely have Fairyland stuck in your head."

"Hey! Over here!" Milo called. "You're just in time. We're doing an obstacle course first. Then there's a scavenger hunt. And tonight, right before the fireworks, there will be a huge game

of Ghost in the Graveyard. We play it every year."

"That sounds like a great plan," Rachel said, feeling excited, but then Kirsty nudged her arm. "What?" Rachel asked in a whisper.

"It's a plan," Kirsty said. "That can only mean trouble. Didn't Skyler say that the magic sparkler helped big events go as planned?"

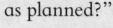

"She did," Rachel agreed with a frown. "But there's not much we can do, right? We just take part in the Honeydown Challenge until we figure out how to stop those tricky goblins."

Rachel and Kirsty were excited to see that the twins had also asked Carter and Sandy to be on their team.

Rose's dad had the bullhorn again, and he was getting the groups in order. Then he announced the stages of the race. "First, you run through the tires," he began, "then you go over the hay-bale pyramid. Finally, you climb the giant cargo net and then slide down one of the ropes on the other side."

"This looks fun!" Kirsty said. "I'm really good at climbing," Carter said. "Just watch me." The obstacle course was set up like a relay. As soon as one member of the team

finished sliding down the rope, the next
person was able to start. There were four
teams, and every team had six members.

Rose's dad stood at the start. "Ready,
set, go!" he called.

Carter started things off. He ran
straight for the tire obstacle. When he
stepped in the middle of the first tire,
there was a huge, muddy splash. It went
up to the very top of his knee sock!
The girl next to him slipped in the
muck and landed with a
thud. Only the
boy on the far
end escaped
without being
slowed down
by the dirty
puddles.

"Maybe it's because of his big feet," Kirsty thought out loud.

Rachel turned to her friend and gripped her hand. "Goblins!" they exclaimed together.

"That's no good," Rachel said. "They're going to cause all kinds of troubles for the other teams in the challenge."

"But what really matters is that they're here," Rachel reminded her friend. "If they're doing the Honeydown Challenge, we have a better chance of keeping track of them. Maybe we'll even spot Skyler's final missing object."

"You're right! I have a good feeling about this. We'll find that magic sparkler and give it back to Skyler," Kirsty declared. "I'm sure of it."

Even More Obstacles

Unfortunately, the goblins—and their big feet—were way ahead. They were super fast on the obstacle course.

Kirsty and Rachel were worried about their team. Carter was a very good climber, but he did not have very good luck. When he was about halfway up the

pyramid, one of his legs disappeared right between two hay bales!

"What happened?" Sandy asked, a worried expression on her face.

"I'm not sure," Rachel admitted. "I think his foot just slipped through a hole."

Carter tried to pull himself out. He scowled as he tugged on his leg. Then, all at once, his leg was free. Carter was

right back in the race, even though he was missing a shoe. Kirsty and Rachel cheered for their teammate, but the goblin was already on the next obstacle—the cargo net.

As soon as Carter had escaped his troubles, the girl next to him had the same problem, but in a different place.

"Why are there so many holes in the hay?" Milo asked. "It doesn't seem safe."

Of course, the goblin who was racing had bounded straight up the bales like they were a simple jungle gym. His feet didn't slip through any holes.

"I smell something fishy," Rachel whispered to Kirsty, but Sandy overheard her.

"Fishy?" Sandy asked. "It might be me. I had fish sticks for dinner last night."

Rachel and Kirsty smiled at each other, but they took note. They would have to be careful with Sandy around.

Carter made up a lot of time, and he was soon sliding down the rope from the very top of the cargo net. It was time for someone else to start the relay.

"You're next," Arlo said to Rachel.

"Wish me luck," she said, and she took off as soon as Carter landed.

First was the tire obstacle. Rachel got just as messy as Carter, splashing through the tires, but she didn't slow down. She was very careful as she came to the

pyramid. She remembered where the other racers had trouble and stayed away from those spots. Rachel made great time and was almost at the top when she felt something pull at her foot.

"What's that?" she mumbled to herself. She tried to climb to the next bale, but the tug came again.

"You can do it, Rachel!" she heard Kirsty yell.

Rachel gave her foot a yank, but she couldn't move. Then, all at once, she started to sink through the hay. Her whole body scraped through the prickly edges, and she landed with a thud on the ground. She was *inside* the pyramid, and it was dark.

"Hello?" she said in a small voice, but no one answered. "Who's there?" Rachel

pushed herself
to her feet. She
felt very alone,
although she
had a bad
feeling that
she was not.

Suddenly, she heard a different sound.
It was a rustling. She looked up and
saw a bright sliver of sky overhead. It
was the crack where she had fallen
through the hay.

"Rachel?" a voice called. Then a face
peeked in, covering the crack. It was
Kirsty!

Kirsty eased through the gap and
landed on her feet.

"What are you doing here?" Rachel

asked. "We can't have two people on the course at the same time. It's a relay."

"But the relay isn't really that important," Kirsty said. "Remember?"

Of course Kirsty was right. Rachel knew that.

"I thought I should help you get out of here," Kirsty said. "I didn't think it would be so dark. Luckily, Arlo is coming with a rope."

Hmm, hmm.

"What was that?" Kirsty asked.

Hmm, hmm, the sound came again, followed by a deep breath. "It's me," someone said. "From the parade. The one with the great dress and the wig."

"Oh, you scared us!" Rachel said, remembering the goblin that Skyler had

helped. "I thought you were a ghost or something."

"Oh no! I hate ghosts. So do all my friends," the goblin said. "I just wasn't sure it was you before, so I didn't say anything."

"What are you doing in here?" Kirsty asked.

"Well, it's a long story," the goblin

said. "They told me I had to stop the other teams, but I didn't want to."

"That's awful!" Rachel insisted. "That's cheating!"

"I'm sorry," the goblin said. "But I can help you out."

"Help?" Rachel felt her heart flutter with hope. Would he tell them where the magic sparkler was?

"You don't need a rope to get out," he said. "There's a secret door."

Rachel sighed. He wasn't going to tell them where the sparkler was, but escaping the hay pyramid was a start at least.

"Watch," the goblin said. The girls heard the sound of something being scooted across the ground. A block of light appeared. The goblin kneeled down and stuck his head in the hole.

"I really loved that costume yesterday," he said. "It was so nice of you to share it." When he crawled back out, the girls could see there was a smile on his face. "It's all clear," he whispered. "You should go now. Quick! And take this."

He placed something in Rachel's hand. It was Carter's shoe.

Scavengers!

The girls quickly thanked the goblin, and snuck back to their team.

"How did you get here?" Milo whispered when he saw them. "Everyone thinks you're still in the pyramid."

The girls explained that they found an exit. They did not explain that a goblin had showed it to them! After all, none of

their teammates even knew that goblins really existed.

"Don't worry about not finishing the course. It's not a big deal," Arlo said. "Those guys in the tracksuits won." He motioned to the goblins, who were still jumping with joy.

"That team was so far ahead that they called off the rest of the race." Sandy pouted. "I didn't even get my turn," she complained.

"But it's time for the scavenger hunt," Arlo said. "And we have our first clue."

WHERE DOES THE BREAD RISE BEFORE YOU DO?

"That's a weird clue," Sandy said. "How do they know when I get up?"

"Maybe this is a place that opens up really early, every day," Rachel suggested.

"And a place that makes bread," Kirsty hinted.

"Muffin Mecca!" the twins chanted together. "We love that place, and they open super early."

The rest of the team agreed, and they all headed down Main Street.

When they arrived, the smell of delicious bread told them they were in the right place.

As they opened the door, a bell rang. The baker appeared, wearing his crisp

white hat. "Hello! What can I get for you?"

"We were wondering if you might have a clue for the scavenger hunt," Kirsty said with a sweet smile.

"I do," the baker said, returning the smile. "For you, I have a clue and muffins, too."

The team left the shop happy. The blueberry oat muffins the baker had

given them almost melted in their mouths. Kirsty held out the clue, so everyone could read.

**WHERE DOES THE TIME GO?
IN HONEYDOWN, IT WINDS UP
AND WINDS DOWN HERE.**

"That's got to be at the old clock in town," Carter said. "It's just down the road."

When they arrived, they looked all around the old building and the tower.

"I don't see anything," Sandy said.

"Well, the word 'wind' was in the clue," Rachel reminded them. "Is this clock old enough that someone has to wind it? Can we get in the tower?"

"That's a good idea," Milo said. "Let's check."

They ran around to the back of the building and found a door. It was old and red and creaked when it opened.

They ran up the steps. At the top, they saw big, turning gears. Next to a crank was a large sign.

**THE SPARKS START HERE!
AT LEAST, THEY DID ONCE
UPON A TIME.**

"Oh! It sounds like a fairy tale," Sandy said.

"I don't think it's a fairy tale," Arlo admitted. "I think it's more like history."

"History is cool, too," said Carter. "I like museums."

"Carter, you're exactly right!" Kirsty cheered. "The answer must be the Fireworks Factory Museum. It used to be a factory where fireworks were made."

"I'll bet we're the first to figure that out," Sandy announced, proudly putting her hands on her hips.

But at that moment, they heard cackles and the scurry of big feet. There was the sound of a stampede on the tower steps.

"Someone else was here!" Milo said.

"Spying!" Arlo added.

"Goblins!" Rachel whispered to Kirsty. The two girls stepped away from the group. "They sure are enjoying the

Honeydown
Challenge, but
they're not making
it much fun for
anyone else."

"Skyler would say
that it's probably
a sign," said
Kirsty. "They're messing with plans.
Maybe they have the magic sparkler
with them!"

"We've got to get it," Rachel said with
a determined look on her face. "I'm
really looking forward to those fireworks."

"So is my dad," Kirsty said, looking
serious.

"Do you guys have a secret plan?"
Milo asked. "If so, clue us in."

"Not really," Rachel admitted. "We

just think we should race to the Fireworks
Factory Museum."

"You're right," Carter said.

"So let's go!" the twins said together,
and the team took off.

The team stopped at the gate and took
a long look. The Fireworks Factory
Museum did not look like a real factory. It
was old and made of wood.

"This place looks like it could easily
burn down," Arlo noted. "It would only
take one spark."

"Well, they didn't *set off* fireworks here,"
his brother said. "They just made them."

"The fireworks they made here were
famous," Kirsty added. "Half the town
of Honeydown worked here a long
time ago."

"You kids here on that scavenger hunt?" a man in the ticket booth asked. He had a long white mustache and tiny round glasses.

"Yes, we are," Kirsty said, walking toward the booth.

"Then you get in for free," he said.

"Thank you," the group said all together.

"Well, you're welcome," he answered, handing them a map and six tickets. "You're much more polite than that group wearing matching tracksuits. They just ran straight in without saying anything."

Kirsty and Rachel exchanged a glance.

"Good luck to you," the man said. "Just look at that map if you need anything."

The group headed through the gate and entered the brass doors. "So, we know those other guys beat us here," Milo said. "We just have to find the next clue first."

"Where should we look?" Arlo wondered.

At that moment, Rachel saw something flash in the corner of her eye. But it didn't just flash, it sparkled! *"Psst. Psst."* She motioned to Kirsty. "I think I saw the magic sparkler," she said.

"Maybe we should split up," Kirsty suggested quickly. "We'll go that way." She pointed down the hallway.

"Of course," Sandy said. "Carter and I will go that way." She pointed in the opposite direction.

The twins decided they'd go up to the second floor.

Before they separated, Kirsty gave the map to Sandy.

"Just call if you find anything," Sandy said. "We're all in this together."

"We will," Kirsty said. She gave Rachel a knowing look. The best friends both knew there were some things that they needed to do on their own.

Firecracker Fake Out

Rachel and Kirsty picked up their pace, jogging down the long hall. The museum had lots of pictures on the walls. There were also a lot of long tables with old papers and tall piles of colorful tubes.

"Are those old fireworks?" Rachel wondered out loud.

"I think so," Kirsty replied.

"I'm not sure this is safe," said Rachel. "If what I saw was a sparkler, it is very dangerous that it is lit in here. It wouldn't take much to set off an old firework."

Kirsty immediately understood what her friend was saying. "You're right," she said. "But it's Skyler's *magic* sparkler. I'm sure it is safe. There's no way it would light these fireworks."

"I wish that were true."

The girls stopped in their tracks, trying to find the owner of the voice.

"Skyler!" they exclaimed, finally

 spotting her near one of the fireworks displays. "It's so good to see you," Rachel said.

"It's good to see you, too," said the fairy. "I've been trying to find my sparkler. I think it's somewhere in the museum. You think you saw it?"

"Yes," Rachel said. "But only out of the corner of my eye."

"I'm sure those goblins with my sparkler are still here somewhere," Skyler assured them. "Unfortunately, it isn't acting like it should."

"What do you mean?" Kirsty asked.

"Well," Skyler began to explain, "my sparkler is magical. Even when it is lit, it is very safe. It won't burn anyone or set anything on fire, as long as I am the one who is holding it."

"What happens when someone else has it?" Rachel asked with concern.

"I can't be sure," Skyler said. "But I do

know that I had to put out a couple of small fires between the clock tower and the factory."

"That's terrible!" Kirsty exclaimed.

"I know!" Skyler agreed. "We have to get our hands on my sparkler as soon as we can! We really need to get it out of this building. With all these fireworks, it's extra dangerous in here."

Kirsty and Rachel looked at each other. They knew that the fireworks were all old, but it paid to be safe.

Skyler took a perch on Kirsty's shoulder, and they began to track down the goblins. "They can't be that far," Rachel

murmured. "I think I can hear them stomping around."

The two girls and one fairy peeked around a corner. Right next to a wall of old barrels, the goblins were arguing. It looked like each goblin wanted a turn with the sparkler. They were all grabbing at it, but the goblin who had it kept yanking it away.

"This might not be that easy," Skyler admitted.

"They got along much better when they were focused on winning the Honeydown Challenge," Kirsty commented.

"Yes, they worked together much better then," added Rachel.

At that moment, they heard their names. Sandy and Carter were calling for them.

"Oh no!" Kristy said. "The goblins will hear!"

"Wait," Skyler said, putting a finger to her chin. "This could be a good thing. Maybe your teammates will help distract the goblins. Let's see what they want."

"Kirsty! Rachel!" the calls were getting louder. Soon, Sandy and Carter ran up to them. "Look! We found the next clue!" Carter announced.

"What? How?" the girls wondered.

"It was on the map that you gave me," Sandy said. "The man in the ticket booth must have written it there."

"That's amazing!" Rachel said.

"Arlo and Milo are waiting for us downstairs," Sandy said. "Come quick! Before someone follows us!" The two raced for the stairs.

Kirsty and Rachel hesitated. Then they heard the tiny flutter of fairy wings behind them. "The goblins heard everything!" Skyler declared. "They're already sneaking up behind us. This might be the fastest way to get them out of here."

It sounded like it might work. Skyler slipped into Rachel's pocket, and the girls rushed off after their teammates.

Rachel sneaked glances over her

shoulder as they ran. She wanted to
make sure the greedy goblins were
behind them. The one with the sparkler
was in front. All the others were trying
to keep up.

After they had left the museum and
were back on the trail, the six teammates
stopped to catch their breath.

"What's the next clue?" Kirsty asked.

FLOWERS WILL EXPLODE
AND THE SKY WILL QUAKE.
MEET EVERYONE DOWN
BY THE LAKE.

"Exploding flowers and quaking skies? They're talking about fireworks, right? So we just go to the lake?" Rachel wondered. "Or is it a trick?"

"I doubt it," Milo said. "The sun is setting. The Ghost in the Graveyard game is going to start soon. We usually play close to the lake, so it makes sense."

With that, the group headed off again. They took the path that led to a clearing by the still lake. They were speedy. Kirsty was sure they were all thinking about the scavenger hunt. They wanted to win! She guessed that Rachel was the

only one who also heard the scampering footsteps behind them. The goblins were right on their tail.

Rose's dad greeted them. He was in the picnic area by the lake. He told them that they had won the scavenger hunt! Now they were tied with the tracksuit team.

"That means if we can win Ghost in the Graveyard, we'll end in first place," Arlo said.

"So what do we get if we win?" Sandy asked, her eyes bright.

"We win bragging rights as the best team in the Honeydown Challenge!" Milo said. "There's no prize money, or anything."

Sandy looked disappointed, but there was not any time to complain. The last phase of the Challenge was starting!

The girls joined their team to hear the rules. One group would be the ghosts and spread out into the woods to hide. Everyone else's job was to search for the ghosts. Each team would take turns being the ghosts, and the group that evaded the ghost hunters the longest would win.

No one knew that the girls were looking for goblins, too! After a few rounds, it was finally time for Rachel and Kirsty's team to be the ghosts.

"This is kind of spooky," Rachel said, looking into the gloomy night. They had quickly dashed off together hoping to finally spot Skyler's sparkler. There were

crooked old trees, loud bird squawks, and the crackle of breaking sticks as their teammates crept through the woods to find hiding places.

"I agree," Kirsty said. "But it's also kind of fun."

Suddenly, Kirsty heard a big splash. The two friends hurried to the edge of the lake. In the dim light, they could see

several figures on the old swimming
dock. They were all leaning forward
with their hands on their hips. Their long
noses nearly touched as they argued.

Rachel counted four goblins . . . and
one sparkler.

Boom, Bang, Sizzle, Cheer!

"How did they get out there?" Kirsty wondered. The swimming dock was way out in the lake.

"Look! They took canoes," Rachel pointed out. There were two canoes floating near the dock. "But why are they out there? Isn't that where they are setting off the fireworks later? And aren't all the fireworks already on the dock?"

Kirsty looked closer and realized her friend was right. There were several bundles and some crates. It looked like a lot of equipment.

"Oh no. Oh no, oh no, oh no," Skyler mumbled as she flew out of Rachel's pocket. "This isn't good. If they aren't careful, they could set off every last firework. That would be very dangerous!"

"And very sad," Kirsty added. "They really will ruin everyone's plans." Kirsty thought about her parents. They were so excited to sit down and enjoy the fireworks as a family,

but they weren't even here yet. Neither were Gramps and Gran. It was one of their favorite Honeydown traditions.

"We have to get it back," Skyler said.

Just then, the girls were reminded that there was a game of Ghost in the Graveyard in the works. They heard the playful calling, and the ghostlike yowls.

"I have an idea," Rachel said. "It's pretty silly, but it just might work."

Moments later, Skyler promised to change Rachel and Kirsty into fairies. With just a twirl of her wand, swirls of glitter whooshed around the girls and they shrunk to the size of fairies. Plus, they grew beautiful, shiny wings. Now those wings carried them over the lake, so they could get as close to the

goblins as possible—
without being
seen, of
course.

The three
fairies landed
in a canoe.
From there, they
could see the four goblins.
The sparkler lit their angry green faces.
Not one of them was happy. They all
wanted the sparkler!

"So, you ready to give it a try?"
Rachel asked.

"Absolutely," Skyler answered. Kirsty
gave a nod.

On the count of three, the three fairies
began to make their spookiest, most

haunting ghost sounds ever. *Wooooooo, woooooOOOO, wOOOOOOOOOoooo.*

The four goblins stopped bickering and began shaking in their shoes.

Next, Skyler pointed her wand at Kirsty. When Kirsty began to speak, sparkles spun in a tunnel around her mouth. Kirsty's voice came out as a deep groan, almost like a monster. It even frightened Rachel!

"*I'm the ghost of the fireworks factory. You must give back the magic sparkler now!*" Kirsty said. "*I will haunt whoever has stolen the sparkler!*"

At once, the goblin with the wand tried to give it to the goblin next to him. That goblin took it, but then passed it off to the one next to him. "Not me, not me!" that goblin screamed, and then he threw the sparkler up in the air.

Quick as lightning, Skyler went after it. She darted straight up and grasped her final magic object. As soon as it was in her hands, the sparkler shot out a burst of rainbow color before shrinking down to Fairyland size. "Woo-hoo!" Skyler yelped with joy. "I'll make this the most spectacular fireworks show this sweet town has ever seen!"

As she whirled in the sky,
happy blasts of fireworks
poured from her wand,
landing on the
equipment set up
on the dock. As
the magic sparkles
faded, the equipment
glowed with magic.

Kirsty and Rachel blinked to find
that Skyler's blast of magic had sent them
back to the edge of the lake and returned
them to human form. From there, they
could see that the goblins had all jumped
off the dock and were swimming to
shore. Skyler was nowhere to be seen.
Rachel and Kirsty were certain she had
returned to Fairyland, so the magic
sparkler was safe and sound.

When the two friends walked out of
the woods, everything seemed very quiet.
"There they are!" a voice cried. "No one
found them! Their team won!"

Sandy, Carter, Milo, and Arlo raced
toward them. "Where were you?" they
asked. "People looked everywhere!"

"I told them you probably hid in the
lake," Sandy declared.

"Not exactly," Kirsty replied.

"So, we won?" Rachel asked.

"Yes!" Carter yelled with glee.

"But we don't get anything," Sandy huffed again.

That's when Rachel felt something tingle in her sweater pocket. She reached in and pulled out a golden charm. It hung from a long chain and was in the shape of a sparkler. In the moonlight, it really seemed to glitter. Rachel was certain Skyler had put it there.

"Here," Rachel said. "You can have this." Kirsty smiled at her.

Sandy's eyes grew wide. "Really?" she asked. She reached out and took the charm in her hand.

"Really," Kirsty said. "It was fun being teammates with you."

Rose's dad promised the winning team extra popcorn, and then everyone went

to find their families for the
big fireworks show.

"Mom, Dad!"
Kirsty cried when
she saw her parents.
They were carrying
blankets and beach
chairs. Gran had a full bag of snacks.

"It's so good to see you, sweetheart,"
Mrs. Tate said to her daughter.

"I'm almost as excited to see you as I
am to see these fireworks," Mr. Tate
added. "And that's saying something."

Everyone laughed, especially Kirsty.
She was so relieved that Skyler had all
her magic objects again.

"Thanks so much for having me,"
Rachel said to the Tate family. "I love
Honeydown. We've had a great time."

Kirsty smiled. "Thanks for coming, Rachel," said Kirsty. "It wouldn't be the same without you." The friends knew it was true. They were a real team when it came to helping the fairies. Kirsty sat down and patted the blanket so Rachel would sit, too.

"I have a feeling these will be the best fireworks yet," Mr. Tate said as the first few flashes lit up the sky.

"What makes you think that?" Gramps asked.

"Well, it is Honeydown's big birthday," Kirsty's dad answered. "But it's something more than that. There's just something magical in the air."

Rachel and Kirsty smiled. The two best friends certainly agreed with that.